THE BERENSTAINS' B BOOK

GROLIER
BOOK CLUB EDITION

THE BERENSTAINS' B BOOK

A Bright & Early Book

RANDOM HOUSE / NEW YORK

 Trade Edition: ISBN: 0-394-82324-9. Library Edition: ISBN: 0-394-92324-3. Library of Congress Catal
Card Number: 78-158387. Manufactured in the United States of America.

W X 6 7 8 9

Big

brown

Big brown bear

brown bear,

blue bull

Big brown bear,

blue bull,

beautiful baboon

Big brown bear,

blue bull,

beautiful baboon

blowing bubbles...

Big brown bear, blue bull,
beautiful baboon
blowing bubbles
biking backward . .

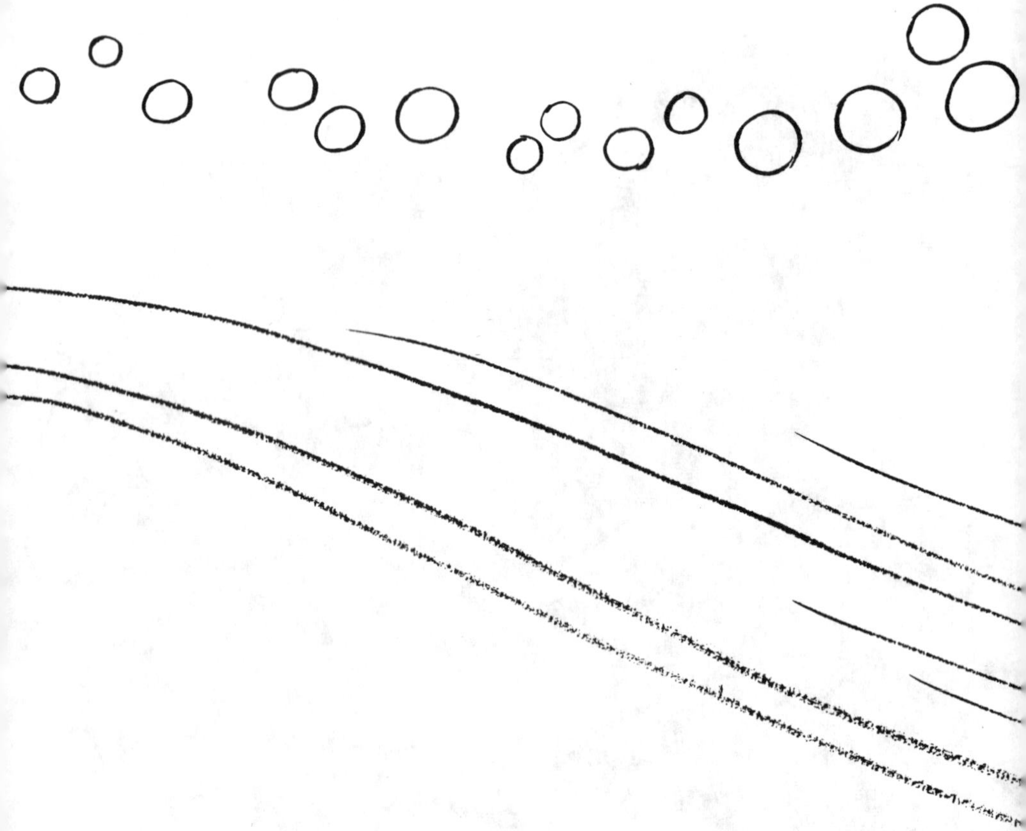

Big brown bear, blue bull,
beautiful baboon
blowing bubbles
biking backward,

bump...

B

Big brown bear,
blue bull, beautiful baboon
blowing bubbles biking backward,
bump black bug's
banana boxes . . .

Big brown bear,
blue bull,
beautiful baboon
blowing bubbles
biking backward,
bump black bug's
banana boxes **and**
Billy Bunny's
breadbasket...

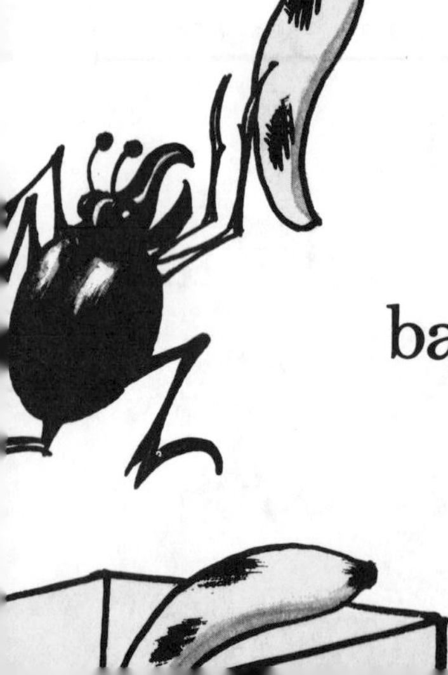

Big brown bear,
blue bull,
beautiful
baboon
blowing bubbles
biking backward,
bump
black bug's
banana boxes
and
Billy Bunny's
breadbasket
and...

Brother Bob's

baseball bus...

BOOM
BUGLE

Big brown bear,
blue bull, beautiful baboon
blowing bubbles biking backward,
bump black bug's banana boxes **and**
Billy Bunny's breadbasket **and**
Brother Bob's baseball bus **and**
Buster Beagle's banjo-
bagpipe-bugle band...

and

that's

what...

BEAGLE'S
BAGPIPE
BAND

broke Baby Bird's balloon.